Robert and the
Attack of the
Giant Tarantula

Also by Barbara Seuling

Oh No, It's Robert

Robert and the Attack of the Giant Tarantula

by Barbara Seuling
Illustrated by Paul Brewer

A LITTLE APPLE BOOK

SCHOLASTIC INC.

New York Toronto London Auckland Sydney
Mexico City New Delhi Hong Kong

No part of this publication may be reproduced in whole or in part, or stored in a retrieval system, or transmitted in any form or by any means, electronic, mechanical, photocopying, recording, or otherwise, without written permission of the publisher. For information regarding permission, write to Carus Publishing Company, Inc., 315 Fifth Street, Peru, Illinois 61354.

ISBN 0-439-23545-6

12 11 10 9 8 7 6 5 4   1 2 3 4 5 6/0

Printed in the U.S.A.
First Scholastic printing, April 2001

For Audrey, who watched Robert grow
—B. S.

For Mom
—P. B.

Contents

Half-Price Special

*S*quoosh. Robert sank into his beanbag chair. His book bag slid to the floor. A book fell out.

"'*Harry the Invisible Dog*,'" read his friend Paul, picking it up. "Another dog book?"

Robert had read almost every dog book in the class library. It was taking him a long time, because he was a slow reader.

"It's the best I can do, since I can't have a dog."

"Why do you want a dog?"

"A dog wags his tail when you come home from school. He's so glad to see you he slobbers you with kisses."

"You also have to walk him."

"I know," said Robert. "I wouldn't mind doing that."

"Why don't you walk dogs for people? Any dog will slobber on you if you let him."

Robert laughed. "That's a good idea." Paul always had good ideas. Robert tore a sheet of paper out of his notebook and wrote:

I WALK DOGS

ONE DOLLAR

"You may have to feed them, too," said Paul when Robert showed it to him.

Robert wrote:

I WALK AND FEED DOGS

ONE DOLLAR

Paul looked at it again. "What if someone has a dog and fish, too?"

Robert chewed his eraser. He wrote:

I TAKE CARE OF PETS
~~AND FEED~~
~~I WALK AND DOGS~~

ONE DOLLAR — EACH

"Should fish cost as much as dogs?"
asked Paul. "You have to walk a dog. You

4

only have to sprinkle dried flies into a fish tank."

Paul thought of everything. Robert tore out a new sheet of paper and wrote the ad over again.

I TAKE CARE
OF PETS
ONE DOLLAR EACH
SMALL ANIMALS
HALF PRICE
CALL
ROBERT DORFMAN
TODAY

"Yeah," said Paul. He got ready to go home. "Don't forget to add your phone number."

"Right," said Robert, writing it in. He looked at his ad and smiled.

After Paul left, Robert made two more copies of the notice. He asked his mom to put one up at the Super Shopper. He asked his brother, Charlie, to put one up in the pet shop when he went to the mall with his friends. The last one went in Robert's notebook for the bulletin board at school.

Robert couldn't wait. Maybe he'd have a dog to take care of soon.

Customer Number One

"*Attack of the Lizard People!*" said Charlie.

"*Nutty Professor II!*" said Robert.

Friday was family night, when the Dorfmans ordered pizza and watched movies. Charlie liked chase scenes, explosions, and scary monsters. Robert liked movies that made him laugh. They flipped a coin. Charlie won. He popped his movie into the VCR.

A band of lizard people was fighting an army of giant grasshoppers when the phone rang.

"It's for you, Robert," called his mom. Robert didn't mind missing some of the movie. It was getting pretty gruesome. Wings and tails were flying everywhere.

"This is Esther Glass," said a woman. "Is this the person who takes care of pets?"

"Yes."

"I live on Oak Street," the woman said. Her voice was shaky. "I'm going into the hospital. Can you take care of my birds while I'm away?"

"Sure," said Robert. When he talked to his parents about his new business, they said that he could only take jobs that were close to home. Oak Street was only a few blocks away. He wrote down Mrs. Glass's address.

The next morning, Robert stopped at Mrs. Glass's to pick up her house key. She was old. Robert watched carefully as she showed him how to feed the doves and clean their cage.

"This is Billie, and this one's Flo," said Mrs. Glass. They looked exactly alike. "I'll miss them. You will take good care of them, won't you?" Robert saw tears filling her eyes.

"Yes, ma'am," he said.

Every day Robert got off the school bus a stop early to go to Mrs. Glass's house. He fed the doves. On Fridays he took extra time to clean their cage and line it with newspaper.

In school, Robert's class was preparing for Earth Day. They had to write or draw about something that was not good for the earth. Then they had to make a suggestion for fixing it.

Robert drew a picture of a truck parked by a river. A man was dumping a barrel of black stuff into the river. A police car had pulled up with its sirens flashing. Nearby, in a park, a boy was drinking from a water

fountain. Over his head was a cartoon balloon that read: YUCK! THIS TASTES FUNNY!

"That's so cute," said Susanne Lee Rodgers, stretching over his shoulder to look.

Robert didn't see how polluting a river could be called cute.

"Thanks," he said.

"You take care of pets?"

"Uh-huh. Why?"

"I have a job for you."

Robert looked up, scratching his neck. "What kind of job? Do you have a dog?"

"It's—"

"Okay, children," said Mrs. Bernthal, their teacher. "It's time to clean up."

"Later," said Susanne Lee, hurrying back to her seat.

That evening, as Robert struggled with his math homework, the doorbell rang. Robert heard his mom's voice. "Susanne Lee! How nice to see you!"

What was Susanne Lee doing here? Robert wondered. He came out of his room and thumped down the stairs. Susanne Lee held a small plastic tank in her hands.

"Hi, Robert," she said. "I didn't finish telling you today, but this is the job I have for you."

The tank had a lid with small holes in it. Robert hoped it was on tight. Inside the tank was the biggest, blackest, hairiest spider he had ever seen. It began to move.

Fuzzy

"What is it?" asked Robert. He tried to stay cool.

"It's a tarantula," said Susanne Lee. "Her name is Fuzzy."

"Fuzzy?"

"Yes, she has eight adorable fuzzy legs. See?"

Robert didn't think "adorable" was the right word. Tarantula legs were definitely not adorable.

"Are you going away?" he asked.

"No," said Susanne Lee. "My cat, Fluffy,

is jealous. I'm afraid he'll hurt Fuzzy if I keep her."

How could a monster spider and a killer cat have names like "Fuzzy" and "Fluffy"? "For how long?" asked Robert.

"Um . . . forever?" said Susanne Lee.

Robert opened his mouth, but nothing came out.

"Please?" She smiled sweetly. "Don't be afraid, Robert. She won't hurt you if you are gentle."

Robert swallowed. "I . . . I have to ask my father."

Robert left Susanne Lee standing in the doorway while he went to ask his father if he could keep a tarantula in the house. Of course he would say no. Then that would be that.

Pets were messy. Robert's dad hated any kind of mess. He was so neat and fussy that he turned all the cans in the cupboard face out so he could read the labels.

"Sure," said Mr. Dorfman when Robert explained about Fuzzy.

"Huh?" Robert couldn't believe it.

"You've always wanted a pet," said his dad. "This is a good way for you to have one. It's small enough to keep in your room, and I'm sure you will keep its tank clean."

"Great!" said Susanne Lee when Robert told her. "Here's ten dollars from my birthday money. It's all I have." Then she handed him the tank.

Robert stared at Fuzzy. Her beady eyes stared back at him. She moved her big hairy legs, and Robert felt his skin prickle.

"Feed her once a day. Here's some food." Susanne Lee held out a box, and Robert took it. He didn't ask what was in it. It was bad enough knowing he had to sleep in the same room as a tarantula.

The Attack of the Giant Tarantula

That night Robert could not sleep. Noises came from the tank on his bookcase. He was sure Fuzzy was trying to get out. He lay there, stiff as a mummy, waiting for the scratching to stop.

Robert was so tired in school the next day that he jumped when Mrs. Bernthal called on him. He missed two easy spelling words on a test and lost his place when they were reading aloud.

"Wake up, Robert. We're on page four," said Mrs. Bernthal.

The next night was even worse. Robert wrapped the covers around him so tightly, he couldn't move his arms and legs.

Scratch, scratch. Robert tried to ignore the sound. He imagined Fuzzy growing into a huge monster—a giant tarantula. She burst out of her tank and jumped onto his bed. *Chomp, chomp.* She chewed through the blankets. Soon she would nibble his toes. Robert tried to swat Fuzzy, but something held his arms down.

He leaped out of bed, tangled in the covers. *Crash!* He knocked over Fuzzy's tank.

Charlie ran in and flipped on the light. "Hey, little bro, what's up?"

"A giant tarantula is loose!" Robert screamed. He leaped back onto his bed, leaving his covers behind.

"Giant tarantula?" said Charlie. "You mean your itty-bitty spider?" Charlie checked under the bed. He looked in Robert's closet.

19

"There's nothing here," he reported. "Did you check your bed?"

Robert flew off the bed. His bare feet hit the cold floor. He prayed he would not step on anything that moved.

Robert's mom and dad came into his room. "What's going on?" asked Mr. Dorfman.

Robert was so scared, he couldn't talk.

All of a sudden, Charlie burst out laughing.

"What's so funny?" asked Robert.

Charlie pointed to the corner of the room. "There's your giant tarantula."

There was Fuzzy, fast asleep in Robert's slipper.

Buster

After that, Robert was no longer afraid of Fuzzy. He even grew to like her. It was nice having company in his room when he did his homework or played computer games. Now Fuzzy's nighttime noises sounded friendly.

"Tarantulas make good pets," he told Paul at lunch one day. He had just finished reading a book about spiders.

"Don't they bite?" asked Paul.

"Only if you scare them. And you won't die or anything." Robert pulled a piece of bologna out of his sandwich and ate it.

"Hi, Paul." Lester Willis put his tray down and sat next to Robert. "Yo, Robert. I found a rabbit in my backyard. Could you keep it?"

"I—I don't know, Lester." Keeping a rabbit was not in Robert's dog-walking plans.

"He's no trouble. I even made him a cage. And I'll pay you."

"How come you can't keep him?"

"My mom says five kids is enough. I'm trying to change her mind."

"I have to ask my mom."

"Cool."

For sure, the answer would be no this time, Robert thought. Rabbits were bigger and probably made bigger messes than birds or tarantulas.

After school, Robert found his mom in the living room. "Mom, Lester wants me to take care of his rabbit."

"That's nice, Rob." Mrs. Dorfman straightened the magazines on the coffee table.

"He wants me to keep it here until he can take it to his house."

His mother stopped fussing with the magazines. "Robert, I know how hard it is to start a new business," she said after a moment. "If the rabbit stays in your room, I think I can convince your father it's okay."

"Really?"

"Really."

Robert called Lester. "My mom says it's okay."

Lester let out a hoot. Robert held the phone away from his ear. "I'll be over tonight. My dad can bring me in the truck."

Everyone in Robert's family liked the big white rabbit. "His name is Buster," Lester said.

"He looks like a giant Easter bunny," Robert's dad said.

24

Mrs. Dorfman held Buster and talked baby talk to him.

"Poor guy must have been in a fight," said Charlie. He pointed to Buster's left ear. It looked like it had been torn.

Lester handed Robert a box of rabbit food. "He also likes carrots."

"Okay," said Robert, patting Buster's head. Lester's rabbit was the closest thing Robert had ever had to a dog.

Robert's Zoo

One day when Robert got home from feeding the birds, his mom met him at the door. She looked sad. He knew something was wrong.

"Mrs. Glass's daughter called," his mom said. "Mrs. Glass is not getting better. She is going into a nursing home, and they don't allow pets."

"What will happen to Flo and Billie?" Robert asked.

"Mrs. Glass would like you to keep them."

"Really?"

"Yes," said his mom. "Your father can help you get them from her house tomorrow afternoon."

What was wrong with his parents? Suddenly his room was a zoo, and they didn't seem to mind!

The next day, after getting Flo and Billie settled in his room, Robert sank into the sofa in the living room. On TV a news reporter was interviewing a man dressed up as the Easter bunny.

Robert's dad came in and sat down next to him. "Well, Tiger, business is booming, isn't it?"

"I guess," said Robert.

"I think you are showing excellent enterprise."

Robert knew that his dad was giving him a compliment, even though he didn't

know what "enterprise" meant. How could he explain that all he wanted was a dog to play with and instead he'd ended up with a tarantula, two doves, and a rabbit?

"Where does the Easter bunny go to fill his baskets?" said a voice from the TV. It was a commercial for Banbury's Chocolates. Robert turned to look and saw a big white rabbit sitting next to a basket with a

yellow bow on the handle. The basket was filled with chocolate bunnies and pink candy eggs. "To Banbury's, of course," the voice continued.

Robert studied the rabbit closely. It looked just like Buster. It even had the same torn ear.

Buster's Surprise

The school bus was coming in five minutes. Robert checked on the animals, as usual. "Good morning, Fuzzy," he said, tapping lightly on her tank. "Good morning, Buster." He looked in Buster's cage and gasped.

"Mom!" he cried. "Come quick!"

Mrs. Dorfman came running. "Oh my," she said. "Oh my, oh my, oh my. Buster had babies."

"But Buster is a boy!"

"Apparently not," said Mrs. Dorfman.

"Don't miss the bus, Rob. We'll deal with this later."

Lester was happy at first to hear the news when Robert told him at lunch. "Seven babies! Way to go, Buster!"

Then Robert reminded him, "Now there are eight rabbits to worry about instead of one."

Lester stopped smiling. "What do I do now?"

Robert wished he knew. "We'll think of something."

"We?" Lester asked.

"Sure." Robert shrugged. "After all, the bunnies were born in my house."

Robert's mom was very clear about what to do. "You have to get rid of them."

"How?"

"Take them to the animal shelter."

"What will they do with them?" Robert asked.

"They'll try to have them adopted."

Robert was afraid to ask the next question. "What happens if they're not adopted?"

"They can't afford to keep all the animals they get," Mrs. Dorfman said. Her voice got softer. "If nobody wants them, they may put them to sleep."

Robert felt like someone had just punched him in the stomach. "You mean forever, right?"

His mom nodded. "The only other way is to find homes for them yourself. If you promise me you'll try to do that, you can keep them until they are big enough to be separated from their mother."

"I promise!" Robert cried. He was sure it would be easy. Everyone would want a bunny.

Emergency Meeting

Robert's mom came into his room with clean laundry to put in his drawers. Bunnies hopped everywhere. One sat on a sock Robert left on the floor. Another cuddled up against one of his dirty sneakers.

"Rob, you've had these bunnies for a month. They're big enough to leave their mother. Have you found homes for them?"

He and Lester had tried to give them away at school. "Mr. Lobel, the science teacher, is taking one for his classroom."

"That still leaves six," his mom pointed

out. "Plus Buster." Lester's mom would not give in, so Buster needed a home, too.

Robert called the Van Saun Park Zoo. "We have all the rabbits we need," they told him.

Next he called Banbury's Chocolates. What if that white rabbit in their commercial was Buster? Robert got a recording and left a message. Nobody called back.

"I'll drive you over to the animal shelter this weekend," said Mrs. Dorfman. "The longer you put it off, the harder it will be."

Robert called Lester. "We need an emergency meeting," he said. "Tomorrow. Lunchtime."

The next morning was spent on special projects. Mrs. Bernthal had everyone making dioramas for Earth Day. She was going to put them on display in the school lobby.

Paul was busy cutting out strips of aluminum foil. "It's for a river, to run through my rain forest," he told Robert.

Paul could get lost doing anything with art. Robert wished he had something to keep his mind off Buster and her babies.

"Can you come to a meeting at lunchtime?" Robert asked. Paul had good ideas. He and Lester could use his help.

"Sure. What's up?"

"We have to take the rabbits to the animal shelter this weekend," Robert said. "Unless we find homes for them."

At lunchtime Lester was so upset he couldn't eat. "We can let them loose in the park," he said. "And what about the pet store? They sell chicks and ducks and rabbits for Easter."

"In the park they'll be killed or die in no time," said Paul. "And pet stores are even worse. I heard that those animals are treated badly. Kids play with them for a while, then abandon them."

"At least the animal shelter doesn't starve or hurt them," said Robert. It made his stomach hurt to say it, but he did.

Lester's shoulders sagged. "Do we have to?" he asked.

"I promised," said Robert.

Lester's mouth trembled. "Okay," he said.

The Worst Feeling in the World

On Saturday morning, Lester was outside his house waiting when Robert and his mother drove up. He slid into the backseat next to the rabbit cage. Robert was buckled into the front passenger seat. Neither of them said a word.

Robert looked in the rearview mirror and saw Lester take a carrot from his jacket and feed it to Buster. Lester really loved those rabbits.

Robert's mom drove to the animal shelter and parked. "I'll come in with you," she said. They got out of the car. Lester carried the cage. Robert walked next to him.

Inside, they went up to a woman at the front desk. "We have some rabbits," Lester said.

"To adopt," added Robert.

The woman smiled. "Of course," she said. She picked up a phone and punched some buttons. "We need an attendant," she said.

Soon a young woman in a white coat came out. "Hi," she said. She looked in the cage. "Oh, how sweet."

With one final good-bye, they left the rabbits with the attendant. Lester ran out to the car.

Robert couldn't remember ever feeling worse than he did at that moment.

On the way home, Robert heard a sniffle. Then he realized it was coming from him.

The weekend was long with the rabbits gone from Robert's room. Flo and Billie seemed sad, and Fuzzy hardly moved. Lester called once, just to talk. He choked up when he mentioned Buster's name.

Robert kept busy working on his diorama of a recycling center. He glued a toy car tire onto a pile of others. He made tiny bundles of newspapers, cut from real newspapers, and tied them with thread. He tried not to think about Buster and the baby bunnies at the animal shelter. But the more he tried not to think of them, the more he did.

Charlie saw him working on his diorama. He came into Robert's room to look at it. "Cool," he said. Robert had just glued three soda cans in place. He had painted them blue and marked them ALUMINUM, GLASS, and PLASTIC, just like the ones at the River Edge Recycling Center.

"You forgot the rats," said Charlie.

"Huh?"

"You need rats in it," Charlie told him. "To be more realistic."

"I don't think so," Robert mumbled. He knew better than to listen to his brother. Once Charlie had talked Robert into doing an oral report about the toilet, and everyone had laughed at him.

By Sunday night, Robert's diorama was almost done. He went to bed early. He was tired from not thinking about rabbits.

The Visitor

On Monday, Robert brought his diorama to school. It was almost done, but he still had to paint in the background.

Susanne Lee Rodgers bounced up to Mrs. Bernthal's desk. "My diorama is finished," she said.

"Thank you, Susanne Lee," said Mrs. Bernthal. "You may put your diorama on the windowsill." It was the first one completed. Susanne Lee was always the first and the best and the smartest in everything.

The rest of the morning passed slowly. In the afternoon, while they were working on math problems, there was a knock on the door. Mrs. Bernthal opened the door, and a man came in. He carried a red cage with the name BONNIE painted on the side. In his other hand, he carried a shopping bag. He gave Mrs. Bernthal a note.

"Children, this is Mr. Dennis," Mrs. Bernthal announced. "Mr. Dennis trains animals. Say hello to Mr. Dennis, class."

"HELLO, MR. DENNIS," said the children.

"Hello," he said. "I brought my sidekick, Bonnie, with me."

Robert's eyes opened wide as Mr. Dennis took a rabbit out of the cage. It was big and white and had a torn ear, just like Buster.

"Some of you may recognize Bonnie," said Mr. Dennis. "She's on TV."

"I know, I know!" said Melissa Thurm. "She's the Easter bunny!"

"Yes, she's the Easter bunny in the commercial for Banbury's Chocolates."

Robert gasped. "It's Buster!" he said.

"I have a story to tell you about Bonnie," Mr. Dennis went on. "We filmed a commercial not far from here. Bonnie got out of her cage and disappeared. I called everyone I could think of, but Bonnie was gone and we had to leave."

"That's so sad," said Vanessa Nicolini.

"Yes," said Mr. Dennis. "I thought I would never see Bonnie again. Then, this morning, I got a call from someone at Banbury's Chocolates. They said someone was trying to reach me. He had a rabbit and wondered if it could be Bonnie."

Robert turned to Lester, but Lester had already gone up to the front of the room. He looked the rabbit in the eyes and cried, "Buster!"

"Are you Lester or Robert?" asked Mr. Dennis.

"I'm Lester," said Lester. "Hey! How did you know my name?"

Mr. Dennis laughed. Robert got up, too. "I'm Robert," he said, looking in the cage. Snuggled together were six little bunnies.

The other children came up to pet Bonnie and look at the babies.

"How did you find us?" asked Robert.

"Your mother told me that Lester found Bonnie and that the two of you took care of her. She also told me where I could find Bonnie and your school, so I could come and say thank you."

"You're keeping the babies, too?" Robert asked.

"Yes, unless you'd like to have one," said Mr. Dennis.

"No! Um, thank you," said Robert. "I was just wondering."

"I have treats for everyone," said Mr. Dennis, handing Robert the shopping bag. "Why don't you and Lester hand them out?"

Robert and Lester gave a Banbury's chocolate rabbit to each of their classmates. Mrs. Bernthal got one, too.

"What do you say, class?" asked Mrs. Bernthal.

Mrs. Bernthal's
2nd Grade Class

"THANK YOU, MR. DENNIS!" the class said.

"Mr. Dennis, will you tell us how you train animals?" asked Susanne Lee.

"I'd be glad to," Mr. Dennis answered. He turned to Mrs. Bernthal. "They're smart, aren't they?" he said.

"They're the best class in the whole world," Mrs. Bernthal said.

As Mr. Dennis talked, Robert nibbled at the ears of his chocolate rabbit. He noticed Paul had started at the rabbit's feet. He turned around. Lester had the whole head of his rabbit stuffed in his mouth. Things were definitely back to normal.

As Mr. Dennis talked, Robert let his thoughts wander. Someday he and Paul could become animal trainers like Mr. Dennis. They could start with Fuzzy or with Flo and Billie. He wondered if anyone had ever trained a tarantula to fetch.

BARBARA SEULING is a well-known author of fiction and nonfiction books for children, including several books about Robert. She divides her time between New York City and Vermont.

PAUL BREWER likes to draw gross, silly situations, which is why he enjoys working on books about Robert so much. He lives in San Diego, California, with his wife and two daughters.